Put Beginning Readers on the Right Track with
ALL ABOARD READING™

The All Aboard Reading series is especially designed for beginning readers. Written by noted authors and illustrated in full color, these are books that children really *want* to read—books to excite their imagination, expand their interests, make them laugh, and support their feelings. With fiction and nonfiction stories that are high interest and curriculum-related, All Aboard Reading books offer something for every young reader. And with four different reading levels, the All Aboard Reading series lets you choose which books are most appropriate for your children and their growing abilities.

Picture Readers
Picture Readers have super-simple texts, with many nouns appearing as rebus pictures. At the end of each book are 24 flash cards—on one side is a rebus picture; on the other side is the written-out word.

Station Stop 1
Station Stop 1 books are best for children who have just begun to read. Simple words and big type make these early reading experiences more comfortable. Picture clues help children to figure out the words on the page. Lots of repetition throughout the text helps children to predict the next word or phrase—an essential step in developing word recognition.

Station Stop 2
Station Stop 2 books are written specifically for children who are reading with help. Short sentences make it easier for early readers to understand what they are reading. Simple plots and simple dialogue help children with reading comprehension.

Station Stop 3
Station Stop 3 books are perfect for children who are reading alone. With longer text and harder words, these books appeal to children who have mastered basic reading skills. More complex stories captivate children who are ready for more challenging books.

In addition to All Aboard Reading books, look for All Aboard Math Readers™ (fiction stories that teach math concepts children are learning in school); All Aboard Science Readers™ (nonfiction books that explore the most fascinating science topics in age-appropriate language); All Aboard Poetry Readers™ (funny, rhyming poems for readers of all levels); and All Aboard Mystery Readers™ (puzzling tales where children piece together evidence with the characters).

All Aboard for happy reading!

To Megan Bryant, the greatest (and most polite) editor any writer could wish for—D.S.

To Adrian and Dorothy, who never eat with their toes—A.S.

Look for the funny worm hiding on every page!

GROSSET & DUNLAP
Published by the Penguin Group
Penguin Group (USA) Inc., 375 Hudson Street, New York, New York 10014, U.S.A.
Penguin Group (Canada), 90 Eglinton Avenue East, Suite 700, Toronto, Ontario, Canada M4P
2Y3 (a division of Pearson Penguin Canada Inc.)
Penguin Books Ltd, 80 Strand, London WC2R 0RL, England
Penguin Ireland, 25 St Stephen's Green, Dublin 2, Ireland
(a division of Penguin Books Ltd)
Penguin Group (Australia), 250 Camberwell Road, Camberwell, Victoria 3124, Australia
(a division of Pearson Australia Group Pty Ltd)
Penguin Books India Pvt Ltd, 11 Community Centre,
Panchsheel Park, New Delhi - 110 017, India
Penguin Group (NZ), Cnr Airborne and Rosedale Roads, Albany, Auckland 1310, New Zealand
(a division of Pearson New Zealand Ltd)
Penguin Books (South Africa) (Pty) Ltd, 24 Sturdee Avenue,
Rosebank, Johannesburg 2196, South Africa

Penguin Books Ltd, Registered Offices:
80 Strand, London WC2R 0RL, England

Text copyright © 2006 by David Steinberg. Illustrations copyright © 2006 by Adrian C. Sinnott. All rights reserved. Published by Grosset & Dunlap, a division of Penguin Young Readers Group, 345 Hudson Street, New York, New York 10014. ALL ABOARD POETRY READER and GROSSET & DUNLAP are trademarks of Penguin Group (USA) Inc. Printed in the U.S.A.

Library of Congress Control Number: 2005016083

ISBN 0-448-44109-8   10 9 8 7 6 5 4 3 2 1

Caveman Manners

and Other Polite Poems

By David Steinberg
Illustrated by Adrian C. Sinnott

Grosset & Dunlap

Caveman Manners

Welcome to Prep School
For Cave Girls and Boys.
Let's start with a lesson
On proper cave poise.

Tuck your leopard skins in.
Leave your spears at the gate.
No crouching, no slouching—
Please sit up straight!

At Wheel-Making Class,
When we meet someone new,
Do we sniff, grunt, and snort?
No! Say, "How do you do?"

In Kindling Class,
If your fire goes out,
We do <u>not</u> throw our sticks.
We do not scream and shout!

And when waiting at lunch
For our saber-tooth stew,
Do we growl? Do we grab?
No! Say, "Please" and "Thank you."

Do we eat with our toes?
Nope—'cause that's just plain weird,
And we don't wipe our face
On our cave-teacher's beard!

And perhaps most important,
Before our time ends,
Let's try to refrain, kids,
From clubbing our friends.

That's all for today.
Now for homework tonight,
Go shock your cave-parents
By being polite!

Percival Pig

"PERCIVAL PIG!" Percy's mother would call,

And everyone knew there was trouble.

"Why, look at this sty! Were you just
CLEANING UP?!

Now come make a MESS on the double!"

"PERCIVAL PIG!" Percy's father would gasp.
"Where did you get this SHAMPOO?!
Get out of that tub and go roll in the mud
Like every good piggy should do!"

But Percival Pig couldn't seem to behave,
No matter how hard he would try.

His teacher would snort, "Were you raised in a HOUSE?

Have respect for the pigs in this sty!"

One morning, a farm girl passed by the fence
And Percival saw she was weeping.

"KATHERINE McKID!" came a voice from
the house.

"You're GROUNDED till you finish sweeping!"

Percy said to the girl, "I can help—
Just show me the way to your broom!"
So she snuck him inside. What a horrible mess!
In a twinkle, he cleaned up her room!

"How can I thank you?" the girl asked the pig.
Percy pondered—"There's one thing, I guess . . .
I'll teach you to clean, if <u>you'll</u> show me how
You made that incredible mess."

So he taught her to sweep and scrub like a pro
In turn, Katherine did what he asked her.
She showed him the fine art of dirtying up,
Till his sty was a total disaster.

"PERCIVAL PIG!" yelled his parents one day.

"What now?" Percy thought with a shrug.

"Why, look at this MESS! What fine manners!" they beamed,

And they gave him a big sloppy hug!

Little Miss Muffet: The REAL Story

Little Miss Muffet
Sat on a tuffet
Eating her curds and whey.
A spider dropped by
And uttered, "Oh my—
What have we for breakfast today?"

As he reached for her food,
The girl cried, "How RUDE!
If you're hungry, I'll give you a bite.

"But NO fingers!" she said.
"Use this <u>teaspoon</u> instead—
Held like this, with your pinky upright.

"Now straighten your back;
Eat slowly, don't smack;
And please do not talk while you're chewing.

"Keep your napkin tucked in
To dab at your chin—
Mr. Spider, HEY! What are you doing?!"

With a splikitty-splack,
He slurped up her snack.
Then he burped, to that poor girl's dismay!

And <u>that's</u> really how
(You know the truth now)
He frightened Miss Muffet away!

The Pickle King

The Pickle King called for his pickles
Each day when it came time to dine.
He'd stack them up high on his platter
And eat them while snickering, "MINE!"

He loved every flavor of pickle

That his Pickler could think to design—

From kosher-dill-tangy to sweet
chocolate-dipped,

He ate every one, chanting, "MINE!"

One evening, the king's Royal Pickler
Found NO pickles left in the brine.
The angry king shouted, "MORE PICKLES!
Tell my people <u>their</u> pickles are MINE!"

A decree was sent out to the kingdom.
The people all gathered in line
To turn over all of their pickles.
The Pickle King snatched them up: "MINE!"

When every last one was delivered,
There were three hundred million and nine.
They burst through the roof of the castle,
With the king perched on top, squealing,
"MINE!"

The sun seemed no longer to shine.
People lost in a world without pickles
Sadly wept every time they heard, "MINE!"

The Pickle King munched several million,
Till his tummy did not feel so fine.
But did he give back any pickles?
No, sirree—he just weakly moaned, "Mine.

As he lay there, he heard people crying.
"Naughty king," he heard one girl whine,
"It's MEAN not to share all those pickles!
Couldn't he let <u>one</u> be mine?"

The Pickle King looked at his pickles.
"Could I possibly let one be hers?"
Then he picked up one plump, juicy pickle
And a new word came out—he said, "YOURS!"

He tossed down that one little pickle.
When he saw that girl's face start to shine,
He shared ALL the rest of his pickles,
And the king felt much better than fine!

The Nose-Picker Champ

The most famous picker at Sunny Day Camp
Was young Lucas Pickett, the Nose-Picker
Champ.

He picked his nose better than any day-camper-

From the Double Thumb Twist to the Three-
Finger Clamper.

Till one day a new girl stopped by the pool
And said, "Lucas Pickett—I'm here for a duel!
The name's Rose O'Flooger from Happy Toes Camp,
Where <u>I</u> am the resident Nose-Picker Champ!

"I've got a few tricks of my <u>own</u> up my nose,

And they're better than yours, or my name isn't Rose."

Lucas laughed, "Well then, how about 'Betsy' or 'June'?

'Cause I <u>will</u> meet your challenge, today at high noon!"

His counselor said, "NO! Young Lucas,
BEWARE—

Don't you know that your finger could get
<u>stuck</u> up there?

Did your mother not tell you? All moms know
it's true!

If you don't stop now, it could happen to <u>you</u>!"

But Lucas was gone; he had followed his nose

To the shuffleboard court, where he stood facing Rose.

The campers were silent as Rose made her move—

A Triple-Lux Back-Finger Synchro-Nose Groove.

The crowd oohed and ahhed. Had this daring move won?

Rose blew on her pointer and said, "Havin' fun?"

But Lucas stepped up with a Two-Nostril Digger

And when the crowd gasped, that boy tried something bigger—

The Full-Knuckle Sinker with a Sidewinder Spin.

The campers all cheered. Rose conceded, "You win."

But that's when it happened. They heard Lucas shout:

"Help me! My finger! It will not come out!"

First, the crowd tugged; the police tried to pull;

The firemen came with a big puller tool.

And I'm sad to report that this group had <u>no</u> luck.

That finger, quite clearly, was terribly stuck.

They had tried every trick and they needed another—

That smart counselor spoke, "When in doubt, call your mother!"

And that's what he did—Lucas told Mom the issue.

His mother said, "Son, all you need is a TISSUE."

I'm sure that you've guessed how the rest of this goes.

With that tissue, his finger blew right out his nose.

And from that moment on, you can bet that boy Lucas

Used tissues—and NEVER his fingers—for mucus!